Hard Candy

Tracy Eire

Published by Tracy Eire, 2022.

HARD
CANDY

Hard Candy

One mile and a quarter North of *Waverleigh School for the Select* there was groomed woodland that ran for miles over rolling foothills and up along valleys and peaks into an area designated as a protected forest. Evergreens dominated the higher the altimeter clicked, but in winter, even the lowlands were an obvious mix of Incense cedar, Douglas-, and Noble Fir, that gave way to Giant sequoia at the heart of the National Preserve.

The same magnificent trees also dotted this particular property. In fact, the weight of fresh snow pushed down their open arms as if the whole tableau beseeched the blue afternoon above Stony Wold Chalet with one question: *Why?*

It was after all, so monstrous a structure its stone, beam, and wood-stained exterior blotted out the most beautiful paths through trees jolly with random colours in the autumn – all for the sake of one family's view. She'd wound down those trails from the other end before... thinking of getting away. Thinking of cities.

Back in reality, there had been 6 inches of snow on Waverleigh campus the night before, and that translated into 10 inches in the foothills where Stony Wold sprawled in Adirondack grandeur. Outside, the faux icicles and stars were a-glimmer in the afternoon sun. The slab stone walkway up to the front, lined with berry studded yews, was lit and bowed in red velvet.

The lone figure of a girl in an old wool coat and UGGs trudged the way with a heavy, but festive, paper bag in each hand. She stopped to stare at the Chalet with a little longing worming inside of her before she decided aloud, "I hate houses with white lights." She walked a few more steps and noted, "White light people like everybody and everything... to be the same."

She climbed up into this world anyway.

The girl hosting the party was, like her, a Waverleigh School student, but that's where the similarities stopped. The Chalet had 10-foot wood slab doors inlaid with layered glass that sandwiched air in between the panes to insulate the house, and while *Candy MacCann* could have told you all about the difficulties of shipping compressed-air layered glass, up-altitude, into the mountains, *Ivy Chérubin* could afford to *own* that glass. And the huge slab doors. *And* the massive estate. And all the twinkling white lights she could stuff onto a circuit.

Outside, the stone slab porch was bigger and taller than her entire bedroom, Candy paused and gathered herself. There were two choices from here. Go in like a flaming Rum punch because she was 'odd', and 'strange', and not from an elite family of businesspeople, or – she looked up at the white lights glowing around the double doors – have an actual *open* mind.

Ivy invited me. I accepted. That was actually... cool.

"Are you gonna stand out there all day with our carry out? I *assume* you know how to use a *doorknob*." Said a tinny young woman's voice over the door's intercom. Its little camera eye moved to sweep down over her.

Candy set down a bag on the cold stone outside, to turn the latch to one of the tall doors. She muttered, "*You're* a doorknob. I'll use you one day. Wait for it."

The inside took Candy's breath away.

The large rotunda was tiled in diamonds of pale stone, where even the grout was bone white. The walls were pale, polished wood, and the ceiling high above glowed with embossed tin ceiling tile warmly lit by a wheel of hurricane lamps. That was one hell of a chandelier.

All the furnishings she could see, from the benches that mimicked the curve of the foyer to the small table with a massive bouquet of red poinsettias, were of the same pale, polished wood. The whole room glowed. Candy set down both bags of carry-out food, stepped in and turned in place.

Hot damn these people are loaded.

There were a pair of wood steps up to open wrought iron gates that led into a warm wood hallway. She paused to touch the distressed surface with her fingertips.

Beyond her, a girl came into the hall, though Candy wasn't sure from where. She had a face straight out of the Birth of Venus, but younger and floating in a cloud of black hair, now with holly-leaf and berry clips. She was also dressed in a pink Lilly Pulitzer A-line with stylish pleats. At least her feet were bare. She said, "Hi. Thanks for coming, Candy!"

"Thanks for inviting me, Ivy." Candy squirmed a little thinking of her distressed jeans and plain black tee shirt. She didn't have a lot of clothes.

"So, uhm, did you bring take out? Is that...?" Ivy motioned with one hand. Neither girl had moved. "No one has to bring anything. There's no need for-"

The second and third girls out into the hallway were in leggings under wintery dresses. First of them was the big-haired blonde Chelsea Sutherland. She had a pretty plaid dress that hit at the thigh and glanced over Candy with distaste that turned to sudden excitement. "You got the Pinka Bello treats, oh good!"

Ivy turned to look at her friend.

Candy picked up the bags and smiled, "As ordered. Come and get'em."

Two steps and the girl leaned in and snapped both bags away. She turned and vanished back down the hallway, to swerve into a room full of cooing delight.

"Right. *Chelsea.* Hm. Well, okay." Ivy said. "Boots off. Come on in." She twirled a little as she turned and bounced back down the hall where Chelsea had gone.

"Well hell." Candy looked at the banks of designer boots tossed around out here. She took balled-up dry socks out of her coat pocket, kicked off her boots and socks while she sat on the stairs, and changed into the dry ones. She set her boots right on top of the vent where they could dry.

Your classic UGGs were a lot of things, but they weren't really winterized.

The hall Candy wandered through was covered in tall walls of family pictures. The room on the left that people had been vanishing in and out of was a large, den-like space with fawn leather couches, a noble fir in lights, ribbons, and crystal decorations, and the largest stone fireplace Candy had seen. And, with the number of couches, it was possible to sort of... fade into the back of the room and sit on... an ottoman. Since the girls on the furthest couch didn't budge to make room for her, as she walked up.

Not that Candy cared. The whole room seemed firelit and warm. She curled her legs up under her. Another girl brought her hot cocoa and marshmallows, and outside the windows, snow drifted, and chickadees called. She leaned her back to the wallpaper and watched the shadows lengthen outside, dreaming of what it would be like to live in a world *like this one*.

She didn't pull out of the warm arms of that fantasy until the gift-giving started. It wasn't, Ivy said from the top of a natural-edged table, a gift *exchange*. For a rich girl, Ivy was excited. She launched into directions, "Everyone gets their gift... but then we all open them at once, okay? Trust me, I've done this before, and this way is more fun."

Then two girls from the volleyball team helped get the packages out. The taller girl dropped Candy's in her lap and hurried onward – the only indication that someone other than Ivy even knew her name.

Candy tucked a thumb in the seam of the crappy wrapping – it seemed no one wrapped gifts well outside of store personnel – and got inside. It was a dark green sweater, with white tinsel lines along the front. It had multicoloured wool bulbs and lights along its entirety. There were cursive words knitted into the front: 'Rockin' around the Christmas me!' And... she looked down at her distressed jeans, and thought of her short twin ponytails, high and black in sparkly red ribbon bows. She guessed that Ivy thought she was more rock and roll than most of these partygoers. Then again, they didn't even do black eyeliner in these parts. But as Candy's fingers smoothed the wool, damn, it felt warm. It felt like quality wool.

"No fair, in the back there." Ivy cupped her hands around her pink mouth. "*Foul!*"

Well-well. Candy bundled the woolen sweater under the paper and chuckled.

"Hey. At least *yours* is *cute*." Said one of the girls from the couch a little ahead of where she sat. That girl held up what looked like a tie-dyed polar bear pelt and stuck out the tip of her tongue from behind it. "I mean you could've gotten... *rrr. RRRrr!*"

"You two rebels! Stop breaking all the rules!" Ivy spread her first two fingers and gestured from her eyes to the back row. "I... like I can see what you're-" The rest was lost in swells of laughter.

And Candy couldn't help it. She genuinely smiled; aware of a warm feeling that meant she was glad she'd come.

An hour later, the party had split between the pool house and hot tubs, and the kitchen, where there were fewer people. Candy's natural preference.

She stood with a red cup full of Bailey's and coffee in her hand. Her own mother might conceivably have bought a shovel and bludgeoned her for attending this kind of event. Bit of an exaggeration, sure, but *vaguely possible.* There was blaring, big-band Christmas music, drinking teenagers stumbling around singing *loudly* and *badly.* There would've been booze-fueled hook ups if there'd been guys in Ivy's class – actually, there were probably lots of boozy hook-ups going down just the same. "Uh. Where are your parents? And... when can we expect them?"

"Oh, they're fund-raising, Candy," Ivy kicked one of the fridge doors shut with a bare foot. "They'll be in New York City until Christmas Eve, and what they don't know won't hurt them."

"Unless someone tips over a Christmas tree," Chelsea added. "There are sixteen in the chalet and one of them is all Wedgewood jasperware ornaments. Do you know what Wedgewood is?" She made a little sputtering sound to get white feathery junk out of her mouth, and that was satisfying to see.

Absolutely everyone had pulled on their ugly sweaters by now, even Ivy, whose blue knit snowy sky had flying reindeer, and the ornate words, *I Sleigh, Every Day.*

"Wedgewood? I'm gonna go with *overpriced*." Candy replied.

Almost in spite of herself, Chelsea chuckled.

But it was crazy busy in the large kitchen, girls went in all directions, picking up drinks, laughing, talking, dripping water from their wet hair, snatching 'Snowball' cupcakes.

"Ivy, where is catering?" The exasperated girl who tumbled in was Belle, twin to Carol, both of whom had identical disapproving looks on their faces though one was in a swimsuit and towel and huddling out in the hall.

Ivy blinked, "I don't... *really know* where-"

"*Oh.* This is why we can never leave you alone to plan things, honey." Belle clucked her tongue, dipped a fingertip in the frosting of a hot-chocolate cupcake, and stuck it in her mouth. "Give me their phone number and I'll call them *for* you."

Carol took a tray of gingerbreads from the counter and added, "It's lit in the pool house. You might want to throw a hot blanket of food on top of that sooner than later, Ivy."

"Its too late." Called a voice from the hall. "Bethany threw up."

"Oh my God. *Eww.*" Carol pulled a face.

"*You.* Put the cupcakes on trays. We have to salvage this." Belle blew by in a frenzy of brown curls. She'd been talking to Candy, who'd been looking around the kitchen at the time. Specifically, at a dog bowl of water that said 'Poupée'.

Candy stepped in to help another of Ivy's friends take a flat of Pinka Bello 'sugar-plum' cupcakes out of a bag. While she set them onto platters, she glanced down at the sudden face that peeked over the granite counter. The dog's curled tail wagged its whole body. "Hi there. You must be... uh... Ivy, did you name your dog, uh-?"

"Pou*pée*," Ivy's eyes widened in dismay as she went through a rolodex from the counter. "Hello: We all go to the same Private school. How am I the only one who knows French?"

"All right, legit." Candy said. "But I'd better stick to English. What does it mean?"

She looked up and across, almost in disbelief. "*Doll*. How can you not know this?"

"Hi, *Dolly*," Candy bent over the puggle's hopeful face and darting pink tongue. She couldn't help her fond smile, "Mommy gave you a crappy name lah? That's a pickle for a puppy ah? *Good baby*." She turned to hand the platter over to another bathing-suit and had to dodge Bethany who came in and sank down into a chair at the sideboard.

Chelsea snapped up a cup, "Sweetie, do you need expresso?"

"No, I'm not drunk," said the girl. She looked up unhappily. "My period started. Like *now*."

The cake and cookie team screeched to a halt as every young woman in the place switched gears. They started rooting around for something to help Bethany with. Candy poured a glass of ginger ale. Others debated over painkillers. And like a magic trick, someone tucked a tampon into the girl's hand.

"Nah. Not that." Candy scanned the puff-haired girl and noted in passing.

Chelsea straightened and blinked. "Did you hit your head, *McCan't*? She's *on* her *period*."

"It's Mac. MacCann." Candy brought over the glass of ginger ale and said, "Now find a *pad*. Chelsea, look at her."

"I am." Chelsea said. "She looks like she's flooding."

"I'm... I'm not," Bethany put her hands up to cover her cheeks.

But Candy considered Bethany's flushed dismay clinically, "Bethany Clifford? The only girl you've probably ever met who not only *knows* what a *hair rat* is, but makes, and wears her own? Who has some kind of... corset on, and big, pretty Gibson girl hair?"

Ivy stopped to look back at the knot of girls around Bethany, curious.

But Chelsea's voice was flat, "Yeah... I don't get it."

"You don't have to *get* it, Chelsea. Get her a pad." Ivy exclaimed but added a quiet. "*I* don't get it either, Candy."

"Uh, tampons got popular somewhere around the 1940s?" Candy said over her shoulder, "And Gibson girls were a thing in the early 1900s. I mean, bit on the nose, but a tampon's not... *period*."

"Oh my God, it's true. I need a pad." Bethany's face reddened again.

"*Meh*." Ivy said. "Not a problem."

Belle swept in from the hall and folded a wrapped pad into the girl's palm. "There's a washroom just around the corner. I'll take you."

Chelsea tucked the tampon back in her clutch. But she held it up a final time to waggle it in air, first, "What does all this have to do with a girl band?"

People paused for a beat trying to get that one.

When she did, Candy laughed. "No-no. *The Gibson girls* came from some artist guy's sketches of 'ideal' American women. They're not BlackPink or The Bangles. But, I mean, if you lead with a *corset* at a Christmas party, then it might be expected that-"

"*Well*. How *presumptuous* of you." Eve came in from where she'd been leaning on the doorframe.

Eve Pace was nearly six feet tall, close friend to Chelsea, and one of the founding mean girls in the firmament. From what Candy could see, Eve's biggest problem running the Waverleigh girls was, slight, pretty-

Ivy made a brittle smile and interjected the acid, "Oh, I donno, Eve. Tampons have *killed* women. And Candy's guess was *right*. Maybe things are more obvious when you actually *look* at what you're *seeing*."

"Oh, Ivy. No one asked your opinion, honey." Eve exhaled on her way to Chelsea.

"You mean like no one asked *yours*?" Ivy circled a hand between them all. "We're talking. See how that works, sweetie?"

Poupée, tongue out, trotted her puggle self into the hall, where her nubby ears quirked. Though Belle didn't seem to notice this as she came back to the kitchen, Candy glanced at the dog's behaviour in the brief hush.

Then Ivy's cell phone made a tinkle of chimes, and she quickly checked. "Well, thank God, ladies. *Finally,* real food. Catering's here. I'm going to let them in. I mean, would you clear off the kitchen island and open the butler's pantry?"

Belle put up a hand like they were in econ class. "*I've* got the pantry."

Candy moved in on the kitchen island... but she was the only one. Typical. She set her hands on this once happy surface that she was now about to clean, alone, as the only one *fit* to do the menial work, she glared.

There was no way Chelsea was going to lift a finger with Eve standing by, a black hole of solid tugging toward the Dark Side, sans cupcakes, cookies, or any ornamentation except her slimming, violet ugly sweater, which said *JOLLY AF*, amid string lights that looked like... they might actually work.

But it was cleaning off a counter. It didn't make Candy flinch. Ivy had asked for their help to get it done, and, her eyes darted up to Chelsea, *a real friend* would do this simple a thing.

Chelsea's mouth tightened a little in response.

This seemed to cause Eve to turn toward the blonde girl, glance over her, and dwell on the image on the red sweater: glittery flying reindeer, and the words 'Star Bucks'. She gestured at the feather-flocked ugly sweater. "*Oh that's funny*. Swap with me?"

Ivy walked in on the end of that, and said, "Chelsea, don't you *dare*. I picked that out for *you*, okay? Eve's got her own. Now clear out of the way. They're a little late, and it'll take a while to get the crab cakes started, let's go."

Belle hurried back into the main kitchen. "Oh, your house is gorgeous, Ivy."

"Oh! We just had the butler's pantry re-modeled." Ivy told her in reply. "It's got *a full kitchen* now."

"There's a full kitchen... behind the kitchen?" Candy paused, last in the line into the hall. *What?*

"There sure is." Belle said. "Just that it's a galley. It's so cute!"

Candy took a left in the hallway, though no one else did. She paused. "So... Bethany?"

"Oh, she can find her way. No worries." Said Belle.

Standing in the fine glow of wood, Candy felt the draft of the front door as several grown men came inside. Those strangers did as Candy had at first, stopped and looked up and around the interior of that glorious foyer. Candy felt her head cock a little. "Uh. Do you know them?"

Eve glanced and sounded bored, "They're *ca-ter-ers*. Keep up."

Yeah... okay. Candy went left and down through the spacious hallway that led to find the washroom. It was difficult enough. The door looked identical to the fancy affairs that had led, one, to a library, and another, to a piano. She stepped inside. Washrooms. It was a guest bathroom with two stalls, two sinks with mirrors and cabinets – each facing the other – and two claw-foot tubs in their own little rooms. Set between the sinks was a taupe padded bench that held Bethany.

Like the other girls, Bethany knew Candy to see her, to pass her in the halls and sit in a room with her for classes. And they shared a daily homeroom, not much more. But even relative strangers could be civil. Candy stood at one sink. "How are you?"

"Recovering." Bethany had made a compress for the back of her neck. "The medication's kicking in. I'll be right as rain by the half hour mark... uh... did Belle send you?"

"Nope. They seemed to think you could find your way to the pool house, or whatever, through a bunch of grown men I don't think *any* of

them knows – but, you know, they get in the house because 'caterers'."
Candy rolled her eyes. "Like who does that?"

"Uh. There's a lot of trust that goes along with hiring... staff?"
Bethany shrugged. "I... don't know much about it. My mom has a nice
place, and I have a great car, but it's a Volvo, and we don't have any anyone
like that. What about you?"

"I *am* staff." Candy said... and cursed her ability to shut down any
conversation. *Nice.*

She rolled her shoulders in the ugly sweater she now adored, reached
up and twisted one of the short pigtails at the top of her head. At least
the hair was trendy, and her make-up was as fresh as a pinned tweet. But
she wasn't anything like these girls. For example, Bethany's mother was
a lawyer. Candy's mother cleaned *Waverleigh*. It didn't help to forget the
distinction, or... so Candy believed. "Hey. Well... I just thought I'd check
on you. Let you know the caterers are here. I guess I'm not as trusting as
Ivy."

"That was kind." Bethany said in reply.

Candy thought about it and winced, "There's gonna be crab cakes.
Can your stomach handle crab cakes right now?" Seafood? You'd be
'seeing it' all right: Candy would have painted the walls.

But something about it made Bethany grin and nod. "Oh, I can
handle it. Like I said, top of half an hour and we should be good."

"So, can you find the pool... house thing?"

"It's an indoor-" Bethany shifted to face her. "Wait. Haven't you been
here before?"

"No." Candy said. "I'm pretty sure Ivy wasn't aware I was *alive* before
I hit her home room."

"Honestly possible." The girl lifted a hand to smooth a wisp of expert
red-brown hair. "Every year, Ivy invites the entire homeroom to these
things. I guess you've never been in our homeroom before."

"Yup." Candy said, "Full yup." People didn't discuss the fact that
there were two class 'speeds' for girls in Waverleigh. The Ivy-League, as

it was called, and the so-called S.C. or State College. It was a good time to remember, Candy thought, that she was lucky to be in *either*. But it was also interesting to realize that Bethany was on the low rung for the Ivy-Leaguers around here. And it had probably hurt her status to blow chunks in front of the upper-*crusty* girls.

Which might have been why Bethany looked grim as she said, "Yeah, I can find it on my own."

Candy knew what it felt like to be the afterthought, the odd one out, and paused with the door open a crack, "I can wait if you want."

"Oh. I wouldn't want to put you out." Bethany smoothed her pale-blue sweater against the light boning of a waist-trainer, when her waist was probably an honours grad from that obedience school. Candy's eyes jumped to the floating candles and the woolly words *Much Dreidel*.

She turned as she began to pull the door and saw a guy walking down the hallway the washroom led into. He reached around and under the white chef's coat to root in the small of his back. Something about it made her quietly shut the door. It was an odd thing to do. But Candy guessed this was out of politesse, because popping out into a hallway and following someone was kinda *sketchy*. She'd been there.

She turned, "I'm not put out. And…. Look, Bethany, don't worry. Hey. Not one of those bitches can hold their liquor. You aren't going to be the last one to hurl here tonight, and I've got a cell phone cam if they want to mess with you."

Bethany gasped on the way to her feet, almost as if she'd forgotten herself and been delighted.

They both cackled for a moment at that, and then Candy opened the door and let them out.

"You're from the S.C. – the slow-class – aren't you," Bethany noted. "Or you *were*."

"Uh, yep," Candy said on their way down along the back hall that led across the kitchen.

"Just so you know, it doesn't have *anything* to do with grades." Bethany added. "Everything at Waverleigh is about cashflow and influence. Get a bad grade? Go argue it with the professor. That doesn't work, have your daddy write a firm letter. Talk about the money he's putting into the school golf course, or the new library. You've got to *wheel and deal* your way to the Ivies. If you think about it, it's the perfect setting for the daughter of an attorney."

She heaved a weary sigh.

Candy smiled, "So, how'd I get into your homeroom then?"

"I don't care," Bethany said and smiled aside at her. "You should stay."

Candy grinned as she passed the kitchen by. She felt her brows draw down and glanced back at Bethany's careful pressing of her temples. "Well, *ideal*. The headache is gone. That's what usually makes me queasy. Man, I hope they do tempura. Last year there were tempura vegetables *to die for. So* good."

"Which way?" Candy asked. "I'm leading. I can't lead."

She didn't know where she was going, demonstrated by the fact they were back in the Christmas tree room and its blanketing warmth. The Mona, a voice commanded virtual assistant, was still playing the tinkling notes of Judy Garland singing *Have Yourself a Merry Little Christmas*. No one had told it to shut the music off. But it didn't matter. And Candy loved this room.

Bethany said, "That's what I get for not paying attention. But, oh my God, what a mess. Wrapping paper *everywhere*." She giggled.

Candy glanced around, "Welp. I'm not cleaning it up."

"Me neither." The girl grinned conspiratorially.

"*Hm*. Generous of you." Eve said from where she arrived in the large square arch of pine wood. "Ivy's looking for you losers. She's worried you're lost seeing as you've been in the Chalet the least."

"And she sent *you*," Candy said dryly. "What a *gift*."

"You're not trying to *pinch* something in here, are you?" Eve crossed her arms under her breasts. "The MacCann's have sticky fingers, is what I've heard. Isn't your father in prison for burglary?"

Now Bethany glanced aside, "Is... is that true?"

"Nah," Candy managed a toothy smile for Eve. "Not *burglary*."

That shut her up.

"They're here." Belle said to someone down the hallway that neither Bethany nor Candy could see, but who turned out to be Ivy.

"I was starting to think you two got lost." Said the small black-haired girl. "We're in the movie room. There are stockings in your theatre seats with your names on them. *Sound of Music* is on. It's perfect!" She sing-songed the last words.

"*Not* a Christmas movie." Belle groused aloud and wagged a finger in air. "Just because it's filled with joy and hope doesn't mean-"

"It's got a convent and a Mother Superior. You should love all-a-that." Chelsea snickered. "*Prude*."

"I'm taking offence for her." Ivy balled up wrapping paper and pelted it at Chelsea.

"Oh, *shit*." Candy dove for the nearest wad as all hell broke loose in the den, all to the high, hyperactive lyrics of *All I Want for Christmas Is You*.

At some point, Candy went for cover behind an overturned bench where Bethany crouched. She glanced back at the sound of a dog barking outside. "Looks like someone took Poopsy for a walk."

"It's *Poupée!* And she doesn't sound like that!" Ivy called from the far side of the room. "Enough! It's time to put tape in your pigtails, Candy McCann!"

Then power cut.

For some reason, the sudden flicker-blink-darkness of this huge house in the declining sun slid a finger of ice down Candy's back. She stood, silhouetted by the windows and looked across the big room to where she knew, but couldn't see, Ivy was.

"Where are your candles?" Candy's voice pitched low, even though there was really no cause. The firelight didn't illuminate the young women deeper in the room though. The formerly bright and happy tree might have been the Blair Witch for the sudden pall of darkness it cast in the middle of the room.

"And how much you wanna bet *this* is how the Germans came up with *Krampas*." Bethany muttered beside her. "Brr."

Candy smiled, though the other girl couldn't see it.

"Uh... there are Christmas candles around everywhere." Ivy said. She picked up the one nearest her. It was lit, though the flame was low in its green glass jar. She came toward the fireplace, and it was possible to make out the words 'Christmas fondant | *Maison de feu*'.

"Smells like paste." Chelsea pointed at it.

Right.

"Maybe it's the breakers?" Candy added. "Where's your fuse box?"

"I don't know." Ivy shrugged at the unfamiliar words. "We should call the Power company to come help. They're usually quick."

Bethany noted, "When a Chérubin calls? You bet your butt they are."

"Oh, *stop*." Said Ivy. "The number is in the kitchen rolodex. Come on."

"Then we can rescue the other girls?" Belle asked.

Candy cocked her head at the sounds of scuffling boots in the hall beyond, and like a very unpleasant light show, she began to *see* what had been slowly raising her hackles till now. She licked her fingers, reached into the candle, and grimaced as she squeezed out the flame.

"What are you-"

"*Shh*." Candy told the girls. She herded them all deeper into the room, beside the dark tree in fact.

When Belle spoke up again, it was at a whisper, "Why are they running?"

Somewhere down the long halls of this place, some of the other girls let out screams and bleats of dismay, and a man's deep voice bellowed. "Cell phones in the bag! And shut up!"

Candy's nod was grim. In her head she saw the guy fussing at the small of his back. At a gun. She'd seen her dad do it a hundred times. And the lumpish thing on the granite kitchen island that had looked like a... a *satellite phone*, and now this.

"Oh my God," Belle began to quake, frozen in place. Ivy clutched her.

Candy turned toward their shapes in the dark, "*That's* why."

"The *caterers* have *lost it*." Chelsea whispered.

"They're not caterers, *witless*." Eve breathed. She wandered close to the fire, where it was possible to see her wide-eyed fright. Her designer coat and Gucchi bag were still folded over a chair, since she'd arrived a little late. She picked them up now. "I'm so outta here. You all have fun."

"Eve," Chelsea sounded stunned. "Are you leaving?"

"I'll get police and such." The girl threw her straight, light brown hair. "Stay out of sight."

If possible, something inside of Candy snapped like peanut brittle. She strode through the room, caught hold of Eve's elbow, and yanked her away from the couch and into the darkness again. "Look, if Belle has to stand here, knowing those dirtbags have Carol, you aren't going anywhere. Not without a plan."

Eve accomplished her next words with two mighty tugs against restraint, "Why? Not?"

Candy shook her head, "Because your dumb ass could get us all in a world of trouble. And I think.... I think those guys have guns."

Belle made a small broken squeak and collapsed against Ivy and Bethany.

"It's not my problem." Eve broke free, took her things, and, bold as brass, she headed out into the hallway and down toward the foyer to leave.

Candy scrambled to follow her. "You can't do this."

"*You* should do this." Eve turned on her and said at a whisper. "Candy MacCann you've never been like those good-girl sheep a day in your worthless life. *You* should come with *me*."

"Well, I would, but, see, you're a cast iron bitch who'd climb in her Maserati and leave me stranded in a snowbank." Candy told her.

"Then you'll have to stay here with the other maudlins and... *muddle through, somehow*." Eve swirled her coat around her. "*And have yourself a very merry Christmas, fool*."

"Oh, you too." Candy backed away into the foyer, toward the little two-fer of steps. "Hope they don't have guns, mess up that new sweater of yours."

"You're so melodramatic." Eve scoffed as she pulled on her gloves. She set her hands on her coat pocket, automatically, and started to feel around.

Candy grinned as she drove out of sight, back down the hall toward where the other girls waited in a miserable knot but unwilling to do anything rash. Re-entering the room, she went to where they waited, bundled together like discard stockings, stood in the middle of the room. And... she couldn't believe she was about to say these words, but: "We need a place to hide, just for a little while, so we can make a plan."

"Is Eve *gone*?" Chelsea's voice wobbled.

Everyone ignored her question.

"I tried to call police." Bethany squeaked. "But I can't get a signal."

"That's *impossible*." Ivy told her and checked her own phone.

"Possible." Candy confirmed from hers. "Stop throwing that word around."

"But how?" Ivy shook her head. "My dad had people come in with High-speed Internet."

"Oh yeah?" Candy asked her. "Let's find out. Where's your router."

"Our what?" the girl shook her head, eyes blinking in the firelight.

"Where did the High-speed Internet people go to set it up?" Candy forced herself to slow down.

"Uh, all over the house...?" Ivy said. "Oh, but... there's a closet for it downstairs. I'm not supposed to touch it. Ever."

Candy pinched the bridge of her nose. "Yeah, that's your first problem. Is it locked?"

"Uh? The cabinet?" Ivy wondered, caught herself and said, "No."

"Okay, we need a place to hide. Really hide. Just... to have a place to plan." As Candy said it, she wasn't sure if that was what they really needed, or if she was just afraid.

"*Is Eve. Gone?*" Chelsea sounded angrier now. A change Candy approved of, at least.

"No, I'm not gone." Eve hissed from just inside the door. She pointed at the silhouette with twin spikes of pigtails – sure to be Candy, "That bitch stole my keys."

Candy smiled, "Took you long enough."

"Get the hell in here." Chelsea gestured widely, and that drew Eve in.

The scurrying girl was fully dressed for the outside, right down to her Sézane coat and tam. She looked livid as she came into view. Her kid gloved fingers darted nearly into Candy's face, "Give me my keys, you *beast.*"

"Nope." Candy nodded.

"We should just go outside and get police." Eve hissed.

"That's a great plan." Candy nodded. "But can we just think it through-"

"*No!*" Eve puffed. "Give me my keys, you little turd."

Candy exhaled and... handed them over. "Look, Eve. These guys are armed. Think it through. *Please.*"

The cluster of young women streamed into the hall as quietly as they could, with the voices of angry men talking not far away, easily within earshot even if their words weren't intelligible. Candy rushed along, nearly shoulder-to-shoulder with Eve. "What if they see your footprints in the snow?"

"You're *afraid*." The taller girl scoffed. "We need police. Not a little coward like you."

"What if they see your tracks and it makes them, I don't know, move up plans. What if they hurt some of the girls?" Candy looked back at Belle's bloodless face. She was wan. Inches from passing out. It seemed only Ivy kept Belle's sapped body moving.

Eve reached the lobby and sped up to push the door, "Stop being such a chicken-shit. *Honestly*."

Candy followed her out into the sundown-chill, and onto the steps in her sock feet. It was *damned* cold. Her gaze hopped over Eve's head and swept left-right, left-right. Was someone out there? She just didn't trust.

A dog barked not far from where she stood, and Candy backed up and darted inside the doors again. She'd started to pull them shut when Eve jabbed half her body through. She took the weight of the slam wordlessly, pushed out, and squeezed inside again to ease the door shut.

"Oh shit. I'm sorry." Candy caught Eve's wrist and they hurried around the hall and back into the treed room. "I didn't mean to-"

"They have a black van..." Eve wheezed. She threw off her coat in a fury of motion. "In the driveway. Like... jackknifed across the driveway." She slung her boots off onto the carpeting.

"So, no driving out." Candy looked around her, thinking.

Kuh-chung went the surge of backup power as the house lit up, minimally, again.

At that point, it was unnerving to go from standing in the concealment of darkness, to the sudden wash of a single floodlight from outside. Eve backed away and almost hissed through her teeth.

"This is too open right here." Bethany wagged a hand at the room with low urgency. "Do you think we can go somewhere better? Figure this out?"

"No, we're fine." Belle said palely. "We're fine here. We've been here so long, and it's been safe in-"

They'd all stopped and gone silent to hear Belle's queasy whisper, and so when the figure of a man with a large dog passed by the frosted glass window, they were already quiet, if jumpy. It was possible to hear radio chatter... but not make out words.

The girls were mostly frozen in fear and didn't move.

"They have... a guy... with a dog. Big dog." Ivy breathed.

"*Ivy*." Candy broke through the tumbling panic inside. "They're using radios out there. Did you hear? I... I need a laptop. We need to go to a room that's quiet and safer than this one. We need to think and... and regroup. Keep trying your cellphones."

"Okay. Okay." She caught hold of Belle's hand and shook her friend a little, "Follow me."

They went through the hallways slinking along the walls in this order: Ivy dragging Belle; Eve sculking with Chelsea; Bethany skirting shadow-to-shadow with Candy.

They did pass the kitchen, if carefully. But there was no longer a satellite phone on the granite island, and that had Candy kicking herself. If she was right, that would have made a call out of this house *easily*.

Then they took a curving staircase upstairs. It was too open a space for Candy, who gritted her teeth and hurried to the next floor in one charge, Bethany carrying her shoes behind the other girl. The halls blurred. They went into a room full of extravagant bookcases and a large desk, everything a warm cherrywood colour, though the books looked ornamental, as if never thumbed through.

"Mom's office. Big closet. Come with me." Ivy caught a large pillow off the leather couch. It was getting hard to see anything in the growing dimness. Eve and Chelsea, who'd probably been in here before, did the same. Candy hung back to look out through the wide patio doors at the darkening grounds. A man with a dog. So... there could be more.

"What the hell is going on here?" she murmured.

"Candy. *Come on*." Ivy beckoned.

So, she hurried into the darkened closet behind the girls. And... it was the size of a bedroom. A good 10 by 10 feet full of racks of business wear, shoe cabinets, and a big ottoman pouf in taupe velvet. She could tell the colour because there appeared to be a battery-operated light that came on when the jewellery cabinet was opened.

"Oh hell." Said Bethany.

The girls stood staring.

Eve scoffed, "Now, I know why they're trying to rob the place."

"Yet they're not up here." Candy said, and then turned from the glinting cabinet that had no less than 7 diamond tennis bracelets, and that was without talking about the rubies. Rubies appeared to be *a few* of this woman's *favourite things*. "Laptop?"

"Here." Ivy dropped the pillow she held and revealed a thin laptop behind it. "Should be fully charged. My mom likes to use it to read Star Trek fanfiction. You know. Thus, hidden."

"That's your mom's dark secret?" Eve asked. "Star Trek fan-fic? Oh my God."

"She ships Spock, Kirk, and Uhura," Ivy pushed back her hair. "I think. Or... it's her password anyway. All 1 word. Like *Spockirkuhura*."

"That's so harmless." Candy opened the laptop and folded down in the light of the jewelry case. She logged in immediately.

"Well, you know how moms are." Ivy said. She guided Belle to a cushion and set her down on it. There, Belle huddled, too shocked to react.

"It's because of Carol." Bethany got to her feet, found a wool throw, and put it over the girl's shoulders. "Not to pry, and... not that I'm techy, but what are you doing, Candy?"

"I'm looking for the gateway. The numbers represent your, uh, router – like how, when you type a URL, the request for a page is routed from your house onto the Internet, so you can see a site? To do that, it has to go to a gateway onto the Internet." Candy had fetched the address and was browsing to the router to check on it as she said so. Several of the girls huddled around her as she worked, but they didn't really follow what she was doing.

"I can't get it working." Sighed Bethany as she put down Ivy's phone. She'd tried everyone's but Candy's by then, and Candy had assured the girl, her own was dead.

"What are you doing *now*?" Chelsea exhaled as she leaned back from where Belle and Ivy huddled.

"I'm trying to figure out how to call for help." Candy shut the laptop and hunted around for a backpack with some padding.

"Did they do something to the, uh, downstairs closet?" Ivy asked.

"No, or... I don't know." Candy stood and stretched herself out. She'd spotted a black bag and picked it up to tuck the laptop inside. "Wifi is just radio waves. It's... not that much different than microwave ovens, or even the two-way radios 'the caterers' are toting around, just the microwave works at under 300 gigahertz and the radios... they're in the megahertz."

"*D'uh*. Well, Candy, *tell me something I don't know*." Ivy rolled her eyes and then became serious. "I honestly have no idea what you're trying to say. Sorry."

Candy looked at her. "I'm thinking aloud. I mean... don't you ever think things through aloud?"

Ivy blinked, "Yeah, but when I do, I seriously don't focus on the same topics, Candy. I know you like Comp Sci, and it's your jam, but *What are you saying*?"

Now Candy got it. Ivy wasn't kidding around. She really didn't know. Candy squared on the girl. "Okay. Hear me out. I can jam the average home wifi with some tinfoil and an old cell phone. They're doing something in your home network, I'm guessing, that's like that. They did it – had to do it – as soon as they came in. Now, for a house this big, you know, your average wifi range isn't going to cut it. So, you've got range extenders. Think of them like when you need to shout a message from inside the house to, uh, me, but I'm in the driveway."

"Oh, impossible, you mean." Noted Ivy.

"*Jeeze*." Candy exhaled. "So, you put Chelsea, and Bethany, and Belle in between. You shout to Chelsea, she shouts to Bethany – the message gets over to me from Belle. You've *extended* your range. If they've done something physically to block the wifi in this house... there could be holes, points where wifi still works, or the range extenders aren't affected. If you have more than one router, our chances of getting help go way up. And I bet this house is big enough for a couple of networks, if it's not all based on extenders."

"*Great*. How do we find those holes?" Ivy nodded eagerly.

"You could put your phone on wifi and scan till we get one," Candy rubbed her face. "It's a bit hit or miss. And I think the bigger problem is that we can't get cell service. It's one thing to jam up someone's home wifi frequencies. It's harder to jam cell service without a *super illegal* device... or cell-tower sabotage. Those signals are radio waves from cell towers. They can travel T3 land lines-"

"Nope. Still nope. Try again?" Chelsea asked.

Candy slowed down. "So, these guys took the trouble to come in here with jammers. Like, highly illegal, *the FCC will fit you for your orange jumpsuit now*, jammers, in the middle of Ivy's Christmas party. I think this is a bit more serious.... *Wow*, that jewelry is amazing."

Eve, who stood staring into the lights like a zealot, muttered, "Damn, right, little sister."

Finally, Belle's head seemed to be clearing, "They could have snuck around this house... all night as 'caterers' and gotten hold of your mom's jewelry collection, Ivy. Why... all this?"

Candy couldn't help the laughter that bubbled up her throat. Everyone looked at her as she stood with Eve, amused.

"We're laughing? Why are we laughing now?" Belle looked dumbfounded. And a little green.

"*They can't cook.*" Candy ran a hand over her eyes and pushed tendrils of hair back off of her forehead. "I mean, they planned and... schemed,

I guess. They have jammers, and now... they have hostages. But I'm guessing they can't cook crab-cakes. So, they had to do it this way."

Which... kind of argued to Candy that this crew was *cheap*. They were willing to cut corners.

Belle raised a wan hand. "*I* can cook a crab cake. I mean... it's not *that* hard."

Eve snickered in response to that.

But Candy smoothed her expression to peer at Belle's serious face. "If not, we may be able to get around them for long enough to take everyone out of here. Safely."

"Oh, about Candy: *I've got it.*" Eve turned to daub a finger in Candy's direction. "You're insane."

"Stop bitching and start pitching in, Eve." Ivy said firmly. She led the way back out into her mother's pristine office.

Candy's gaze passed over lakeside family photos, and a bisque reindeer on the desk, and paused on the window that looked out on the grounds.

Ivy noted. "The first deer's nose usually glows red.... I mean... the emergency generator is supposed to power the network. Candy, doesn't that mean wifi too?"

Candy reached out and touched one of the porcelain antlers beside her. Three larger white wood deer were close to her height and in a small alcove by a window seat that overlooked the grounds and thickening snowfall. "The wifi needs power. Even if it has that, it's a radio wave, and you can shoot the same frequency back at it to cancel a radio-wave out. If emergency power includes your network, then connecting with ethernet – with a cable – may still give us something to go on."

Ivy sighed, "I've never connected a cable to *anything* in this house."

"Just because you haven't, doesn't mean you can't." Candy looked around but didn't find an extender, or anything with ports for a wired connection. That gave a fateful gravity to her search. There was one place that would have all the ethernet cables and ports she could ever need. But only if the bad guys didn't find it first – weren't in it already. She sighed at that realization and looked left.

The other girls had grouped together around a whiteboard Ivy had produced by rolling wall panelling aside. Candy focused only when the squeak of Ivy's red whiteboard marker broke through her concentration.

The Chérubin chalet was a large and rambling property, and Ivy had rendered it in a decent blockish drawing on the whiteboard. Eve drew a expert cluster of mistletoe with a green marker as the hostess paused to examine her work. Candy wandered over on the tail end of Bethany tapping the front door area and saying, "-because that's an obvious place to post a guard dog."

No one spoke for a moment.

There was an arrow pointing at a peaked box that said *Connected pool house*. Another pointed at a central staircase marked *Main* that ran between all the floors, and a third at the little box called *Internet closet for Candy*.

"The caterers will take the main stairs everywhere, I'm betting. We should stay off those. They probably *don't* know about," she drew a series of x-marks, "the servant's stairs."

"Candy," Eve sing-songed. "*We're just talking about you.*"

"She means the Internet closet," Ivy said with an eyeroll. "Really Eve, you are so *extra*."

"Mm," said the girl. "I think we should hide all your mom's jewelry cases in the whiteboard wall too, by the way."

"Not a bad idea." Bethany weighed in. "*I* didn't know this thing was here."

"Don't worry about that," Ivy turned to search Candy's face. "Anything?"

"Nothing." Candy leaned in to look at the little red Xs. "Servant's stairs?"

"They're off for Christmas, but we usually have some help to keep the place up." Ivy noted.

Candy cocked her head, "I wonder if they have their own network?"

"Carol's here." Belle said into the silence. She pointed at the *Connected pool house*.

"I'm betting," Ivy said. "Because that room opens up to the deck – like it has big, automated doors that are shut off in winter – and you can *lock* the doors to the pool house going in from the main house side. You know. In case you need to use it like a detached pool for events."

It made Candy wonder *How would the bad guys know that*? Maybe they'd been watching and knew that the girls had moved into the pool area? But that wouldn't explain knowing they could bar the girls in.

"Thanks to the catering, the girls either have to stay put in there, or somehow run out in the snow in their bathing suits, I mean... which is just *rude*." Eve said disdainfully. She glanced across at Chelsea. "Can you imagine what 10 feet of snow does to a pedicure?"

"It does *frostbite*." Bethany said flatly. "Followed by toes, like, *falling off*. I bet you can die trying to get to the neighbour's house when it's snowing out here. It's not that different from *Waverleigh*."

Eve understood at once, "Siberia."

"Huh." Said Chelsea, almost to herself.

"What are you thinking, Chels?" Ivy asked her.

"Not that that's her department," Eve sighed.

Chelsea reddened, but still told them all, "If you think of this Eve's way, *none* of us can get out of here, because all our coats and boots are in the closets off the foyer. Or in the foyer itself."

"Another good reason to cooperate with catering." Eve said archly. "Even I left my things in the sitting room because of you fools."

"Cooperate. Sure. Unless they plan to shoot us because, you know, we've seen their faces, or whatever." Chelsea replied. "And what are the chances of that?"

"Yeah, we need to split up." Candy told them. "One group of us has to move the clothes that'll be needed to get us all out and put them...

somewhere we can control. Then the others need to try to get a message out to police."

"There are 25 girls in this house." Belle underscored. "You want us to move 25 coats and, like, 50 boots without getting caught? And then walk... where?"

Good point.

"Any other buildings on the property?" Bethany asked Ivy. "This is a big piece of land."

"Uh. We have one of those steel barns full of my dad's sport's cars." Ivy shrugged. She stepped up and drew it on the whiteboard.

Candy crossed her fingers, "Is it heated?"

"*Everything* is *heated.*" Ivy chuckled, as if it hadn't occurred to her that a barn might not be.

That made Bethany exchange a sympathetic glance with Candy before she said, "Okay. Who should go do the foyer, and who should do the Internet closet with Candy?" Bethany held up a hand on the tail end of her comment, and Candy nodded.

Ivy realized, "I... should do the foyer. I know where we can get other types of boots to sort of... substitute for the mess out there. I'm taking Chelsea and Belle. They know the house without having to take much direction."

Bethany and Candy immediately looked at tall, and intentionally intimidating Eve. The expensive young woman began to open her mouth to speak, but Ivy cut her off.

"*No.* You may absolutely *not.*" Ivy bristled. "Eve's all yours, Candy."

"Yay." Bethany bowed and shook her head.

Eve looked insulted, "At least *I* know my way around."

There was that.

Now Ivy tapped the whiteboard right beside the mistletoe and spoke aloud, albeit quietly, as she wrote. "*1. No one goes near catering staff. 2. Stay away from main stairs. 3. NEVER confront the caterers.*" She set the pen down and dusted her hands. "Those are the *golden rules*. We are a conflict-free group here tonight. Got that, my bitches?"

"Loud and clear." Said Eve over her crossed arms.

"Yeah, sure." Bethany nodded.

"Then we meet back here in 45 minutes... if that's enough time." Ivy dissembled a little at the end. "Having... a bit of trouble gauging a time-frame for taking down a band of armed thugs."

No one spoke for a moment.

"Let's start with about as long as it takes to get-" Candy raised a hand, turned it around and flicked her fingers. Her red fingernail paint glimmered. It was intersected with lines of blacks and greens to make a festive plaid.

"Nail gels done." Ivy nodded. "Okay. Got it."

"We should listen to her," Eve crossed her arms on her ribs and eyed the other girls. "Her father is a *professional criminal*."

Capping the pen that she held with a pop, Ivy chirped, "*Stuff it*, Eve." Then she smiled genially, "*Okay*. Let's be back in an hour."

The tall and polished girl's eyes had opened wide in a moment that betrayed her indignation... but she buttoned-up and made no further observations on their sorry situation, or Candy's parentage.

Candy simply snatched up the backpack full of laptop she'd taken and headed for the door. "Well.... Here goes nothing." But she froze with her hand on the door latch, and her mind churning. What if people got hurt because of what she was about to do?

Try to do.

Ivy stepped up beside her, at the latch of the second door. She whispered, "You can do it, Candy." They stood listening for almost a minute before Candy opened her door.

In the hall, Ivy's team of girls went right, and Candy's split left. No one spoke in the occasional glow of emergency lighting.

Candy eyed it as she walked. As long as the power was down, the cameras in here, supposing there were in-house monitoring cameras, would be dead. They had to move quickly. If the baddies who'd stormed this place felt confident enough to bring main power online again, it could be because they truly had taken control. And she didn't know what that would mean for her side, the *goodies*.

"What's with all the Christmas stocking decor this year?" Eve breathed as they minced across polished wood floors in near darkness. "Honest to God, on *every* fireplace, it's a bit much."

"I don't think those guys are in this part of the house." Bethany ignored the taller girl.

"I mean, what do they really want here?" Candy whispered to herself, and then snagged Eve. They were about to go across a stretch of hallway opposite windows. "Down."

"What? Me? Crawl?" Eve asked.

Bethany dropped to creep across under the windows without having to be asked. Candy did the same. The floors were remarkably tidy. Only when Eve realized that she was being left behind did she drop and follow. Already standing on the other side of the row of glass, Bethany leaned into mutter, "You'd think she'd have no problem travelling around on her belly."

"Yeah, I thought she'd take to it naturally, and just slither on over." Candy replied. "But we should stay till she reaches us. It's dangerous to get separated." She stepped back and flattened herself to the wall to wait. Eve reached them a moment later and hurried up to her feet to dust, unnecessarily, off.

"You mention that to *no one*." Eve pointed at them.

"Keep on dreaming." Candy said as she brought them to the first door that was different than the others in the hallway. For one thing, it was a single door, and for another, it was a non-standard size. It was still polished solid wood, but it was narrower than any of the other doors hereabouts. It also didn't have decorated fir wreaths on bronze over-door hooks.

"Bingo." Said Candy. "The holiday spirit stops here."

Eve glanced up with a blink of surprise and realized this was the only undecorated door. "I'm sure it's just the circumference of the wreath, dear."

"Just like I'm sure they could've managed *a door swag*." Bethany noted brightly.

"*Shush*." Candy said. The door opened to dark and windowless cold that breathed a woodsy scent along her shins.

Even though their cells didn't work for calls, Bethany flicked on her cell's flashlight, briefly, to show a polished handrail that led down white wood stairs. "Smells like the pine barrens down there."

"Right. Shut the door and say *Jersey Devil* three times," Candy felt along the darkened wall, "and a Hammerhead bat will appear."

Bethany nearly smiled. But not quite. She covered the light with her palm, "Uh. So, all my hair is standing on end right now."

"Good news." Candy told her. "You're not alone." She caught the rail and felt her way down the curving staircase in the dark.

The downstairs was a mix of storage and recreation rooms that featured a single, long hallway through which the heat cycled. Trees dotted the way like something out of the White House foyer display. There might have been a theme: *Christmas through the ages*. From the glass candles, bird figurines, and pinecones on the sweeping boughs of the first to the pink tree with candy ornaments and an ice-cream cone 'star' at the end of the collection.

Just beyond was a semi-circle of light. A large hand-held flashlight, battery operated, aimed at the open door of what had to be, "The Internet closet." Candy said grimly.

"Crap." Eve nodded.

They waited. But nothing moved.

"Where is he?" Asked Bethany.

The squawk of a radio sounded in the dark downstairs, but... dimly.

Candy stepped out and started down the hall with her backpack in hand. Hiding wasn't doing them any good, after all. She'd gone several steps before she looked behind to find both Bethany and Eve were coming with her, even if their faces were horrified, and they depended on Candy's slender frame for scant cover.

She eased into the shadow of the door and peeked between the slab of it and the jam. There was a guy inside. Candy turned and pointed at the door a little frantically. Both young women behind her flattened to the walls or sank into doorframes. After a moment of off-tune singing to Jingle Bell Rock, the guy got up from his crouch, and walked out of the room. Candy was too frightened to even move at that moment, but he went down the hallway and vanished into a door several feet along the opposite wall.

Seconds after that, Eve bumped up against her to breathe, "*Bathroom.*"

Right. Not a lot of time.... Candy ducked around the door and into the Internet closet.

It was actually a cooled room with a server rack inside. She looked up. The top-of-rack router glinted back at her to the beat of '*hear all the bells*', it's blinking lights alive, and Candy smiled at it. Once she was inside, it wasn't hard to see where the problem was. Some cables had been pulled – the servers couldn't talk to each other – and some led into an anonymous black box with four antennas. Touch that, and he'd know someone had been here in seconds.

But she was betting it was the jammer broadcasting a 2.4 GHz signal, among others.

The supply cart jammed into the corner was more like an art cart. It had a folded extra ethernet cable sitting inconspicuously among the tangle, so Candy took it. She turned over the mysterious black box and memorized the address and credentials on the bottom as quickly as she could, then plugged into the router and tucked the other end into her ethernet port. The cable could run out under the door hinge and clear down the hallway. It reached about 25 feet, Candy estimated, which brought her several feet into the next room to crouch on the floor. Next door turned out to be a large laundry.

Once they were inside in the light of Bethany's phone, Eve leaned on the door, while Candy got online.

She muttered, "It would take too long, and be too obvious if I were to fix what he's doing." The first few apps Candy downloaded and tried sat with their wheels spinning. "He'd, for sure, know we were here."

She said this as she browsed the networks. She accessed the jammer and... quietly disabled protocols. It was risky, but it might slow him down.

"You're kidding." Bethany shook her hands out nervously, and paced. "We can't fix it?"

"Some of this is locked down like a Reverse Proxy... I bet it started life as a Reverse Proxy.... And I have some info now." Candy exhaled slowly. "There are three wifi networks. One is totally jammed, I... can't get a gig out of it. Nothing. The faster one is slow... slow like... modem slow. The last is online, but the signal is weak from here. I... I think that might be the steel barn." That was the network she'd snuck into, messing with the Jammer's hold.

"Okay." Bethany murmured in agreement.

A blue page flashed up on screen.

"What's that?" Bethany jolted, her hands curling up by the boning of her corset.

"That's the local police department's online Contact page. It's for non-emergencies." Candy said. "But it's working, even if I can't get Video Calling going."

"So, they have a hacker... of some kind?" Bethany said.

"More likely a Network engineer, or... that's what it looks like so far." Candy filled out the Contact page with the address and the words WE ARE TRAPPED IN THE HOUSE BY A LARGE # OF MEN RIGHT NOW. GUNS. NO CELL SIGNAL + IT'S NOT SAFE TO CALL. She copied and resent this mail close to a dozen times. The ethernet pipe seemed... clogged. Full of some traffic or other that was killing her Speed Test, but a few of the tabbed pages flipped from the spinning wheel to 'Thanks for your mail'.

Candy clapped her hands over her mouth in delight. She looked up at Bethany and nodded, "*Sent*."

"*You little queen*." Bethany suppressed her happiness.

"Don't get excited, *neek*," Eve said on the heels of this. She bent over the screen and pointed at the line that said 'We generally respond to the non-emergency line within 24-hours'. "But I guess yours was marked 'URGENT', right? With all caps?" She rolled her golden eyes.

"It's better than nothing, which is what we had." Bethany told her.

Candy froze. A window had launched on the laptop. A message window. It looked innocuous enough, except for the fact it read:

WHO ARE YOU?

"Oh, shit. Okay. I think this is our network guy." Candy told them.

"How long till he finds the cable and follows it down here." Eve said between her teeth.

"It's pretty untidy in that closet right now." Candy tried to calm herself. "Uh. Just in case, could you look for something heavy, like a frying pan, or a-"

ILL FIND YOU.

"Yeah, asshat, try finding *English grammar first*." Eve hissed, but quietly. She was scared and the net result of that was that she was *furious*.

But, Candy realized, they had to stay calm. Especially *her*. *Somehow*.

"It's time to go." Candy shut the laptop's lid. She did her best not to betray the waggles of anxiety she felt roiling in her gut at this stranger – this *dangerous* stranger – catching her red-handed in the dark. "We need to be quiet when we walk out of here. Quiet as mice."

"Where are we going?" Bethany asked from nearby.

"Out in the hall and back to the stairs. We can hide in the trees." Candy breathed evenly.

"She means the Christmas trees, right?" Eve's tone was half acerbic, and half churning anxiety when she said so. She wrung the fingers of one hand in the other, without taking much notice.

Candy tucked the laptop away in the bag with its power cord. She left the ethernet cable because she couldn't unhook it from the other side. They gathered around the door, silent and listening, as Eve held the handle in her quaking hand. Then the tall girl had had enough, as was to be expected. It seemed a feature of her abrasive personality that she *hated* to be afraid.

That, at least, Candy could understand.

So, Eve opened the door in a quick, quiet turn and pull.

The hall outside was fragrant with balsam fir, still, and lit in a brume of coloured battery-powered lights that made tinsel patterns and long pine needle shadows along downstairs darkness. Nothing moved here. Eve started to go. Candy caught her back.

Down the hall, the radio crackled with an irritated voice, "*Charlie?*"

A man's voice replied, "Sorry, boss. I thought I heard something."

The voice made everyone recoil, and Bethany cover her mouth with both hands. Maybe, Candy thought, it was worse to know one of their names as if he could be a normal person, outside of this incident, and not just a faceless monster that had invaded the Chérubin house, rounded up a throng of private school girls for... they didn't know for what reason yet. But a lot depended on *why*. Candy stared into space and wondered... how much she could take before she lost it herself, and what she would do if she ever did.

Charlie exhaled. "Yeah. We've got a problem."

"Everything's on schedule right now. That's not what I want to hear, Charlie." Said the irritated radio.

"Me neither. But maybe I can take care of it." He sounded ready to end the transmission.

Candy looked up at Eve's grey-cheeked face and thought... *how odd.* They didn't communicate very well for a crew.

"*Tell me* what it *is*." Said 'boss', but in the unmistakable tone of 'imbecile'.

"Found someone on the network." Charlie's unaccented tones explained.

His boss sounded sharper, like a New York City thug, "You told me there *would be* no network."

"There won't be. But I'm *not done*. And I found some guy with an IP from inside this network's range wandering around the software like he's checking my work. You gotta know your stuff to nose around where this little shit was nosing." Candy tipped her head a little but didn't dare look out and the speaker.

"Disgusting." Said the other man.

"Tell me about it." Charlie grumbled, and then his voice got quieter, and Candy realized what was happening. He'd either stepped back into the 'Internet closet', or he'd turned away. "Sent back a little message that I was going to own his ass as soon as I was done here."

As his voice remained somewhat quieter, Candy peeked out.

She got a little shock at how tall this guy was, just standing in the hallway in his black caterer pants and white shirt. He still wore the black apron, but she could see a wire crimper hooked over the edge of the pocket.

The boss's scratchy radio voice said, "Charlie, I don't have to tell you-"

"Nah. Of course not." Replied Charlie.

"Can you find your new little friend?"

"I can." Charlie scratched his stubble and considered. "Yeah."

"And do you know what he was really doing?"

Candy stepped out of the laundry room and went across the hall to the white Christmas tree covered in fairy lights and confections. There, she crouched down to one knee and watched Bethany scurry beside her to huddle behind what looked like a match-box car, and Valvoline ornament tree. It was darker there. She pointed at the guy with one hand, and up and down the hallway.

Eve had shut the door silently, again, but wasn't behind the next tree.

Charlie's cough was surprisingly close. "He took me by surprise the first time, and I didn't have a packet sniffer running then, so I don't have a detailed log. He was in command line, looking around. If he gets back on the network before I bring it down, I'll locate him."

Good to know, Candy thought.

The radio crackled, "Excellent news, Charlie. Now, bring down the network, please, before authorities are alerted. Whoever this little wrinkle is, *if* you find it, *smooth it out*. Otherwise, stay on task and do your job. I didn't pay you to chase shadows."

Charlie was far enough down the hallway now, for Candy to sneak to the next, more shadowy tree. She dropped down by Bethany, who cupped a hand and whispered in her ear. "Eve said go."

Candy glanced up at the door across from them.

Inside, she knew, Eve was afraid. Problem was, she couldn't hide there and be forgotten by the thieves in the house. She shook her head at Bethany and tapped a finger on the wood floor before she pointed at the cable that led into the laundry.

She will be caught.

Bethany's lips curled up in a silent bad word.

The radio crackling died.

Candy couldn't tell where Charlie was without it, until he walked back into the closet and the light down that hallway shifted as a result. Not much else she could do but to stand up and stretch her muscles. She smoothed back her hair, needlessly, and skulked across the hall with her eyes on the Internet closet. Then she went into the laundry and found that it looked deserted.

Lessee. Eve's too big to fit in the driers....

She went to the tall cabinets stood back, and said, "Time to leave, Eve. He will find the cable that leads up here, and you'll be here to get caught."

Slowly, one of the cabinet doors opened. Eve was grim, but grateful, as she stepped out. She held an iron in her fist, the cord wound around the opposite hand.

"You were going down fighting." Candy said quietly.

"I wasn't planning on it, no." Eve said spicily.

"We need to go upstairs before Charlie finds the-"

They both swung their heads around when the cable jogged against the base of the door. It made a soft slithering sound, followed by plastic bumping against wood, but gently.

"Maybe he hasn't found it. Maybe he's just moving around in the closet and it's..." Eve's whisper trailed off. She broke from where she stood and hurried for the doorway. This time they opened it with just a dart of a glance outside into the lights and garland.

With the door open, the ethernet shot out and scudded down the hallway. That pull had been much harder by the looks of it.

"What the hell is this?" Charlie exclaimed in amazement.

Both girls bolted into the hall, and neither tried to shut the door, or, particularly, to be quiet. They were like a team of horses: fast, of the same mind, and united by their circumstances, no matter how different they were as individuals.

Bethany broke from cover dramatically, to chase them down: she pushed two thick tall trees over onto the floor and bolted after Eve and Candy.

The noise and shatter of glass made Charlie cry out in confusion and shelter in the closet again.

This let them reach the stairs and throw the door open. Candy backed up and glanced out to see that Charlie was struggling. Yes, he'd stumbled out into the halls. But he'd run afoul of the first tree and fumbled along its length, one-handed in the gloom. She nodded and shut the door at the base of the stairs as quietly as she could.

The guy's other hand had held a Glock 26. Candy knew it *on sight*. Her mother had one. Small. Compact. Powerful. It was a great weapon for concealment.

She pushed through the urge to panic. Adrenaline helped her burst from the bottom of the stairs and sprint between girls right to the top. She stood there with her finger up across her lips thinking, almost willing them, *Shhh*, because wouldn't it suck to emerge into a hallway full of gunmen just having evaded the concealed carry downstairs?

They tried to still themselves and breathe evenly, quietly.

It didn't quite work, but... it was better than their performance downstairs.

Candy didn't have time for more than a preliminary check before she opened the door and exited into the hallway. They could hear men's voices very close by.

The caterers were in *the kitchen*.

Eve held up the iron. *Yes?*

Bethany held up three fingers at the taller, thinner girl. *No.*

NEVER confront the caterers.

List item 3 on Ivy's *To Do. Right.*

Candy didn't orient in the hallway quickly enough or know where to go. She simply turned them away from the kitchen and ran.

"What is that?" Came a question from behind her.

They ran without caring if they were loud now.

"Hey!" Charlie burst out of the door. "Hey! They're in the hall! There's a few of them!"

"Go!" Candy barked. She stepped on a rug and went sailing as she hit the corner. Her hands scrabbled along the flooring. Bethany squealed, loud and high, and caught hold of Candy, double-fisted.

The bullet, when it struck, split the white pine wall panelling and created a confetti of splinters in air like: *Congratulations, you survived your first gunman*! Candy didn't know much about the world for a moment after it hit. She'd fallen on her side and didn't even feel it when Bethany hooked a hand under her arm and dragged her down the wood flooring of the next hallway, basically, on her tush.

She kicked to her feet, flipped over onto her knees, and went on her hands and sock-feet up the back stairs, laptop bag smacking her in the back of the head the whole way.

None of the girl's made a sound apart from breathing and running.

Candy was in a strange, suspended state where she was unable to think of anything beyond deep urgency and speed. Like a crème rinse for her dark hair, the gunshot had washed away every spot of sense in her head, and it wasn't restored until Eve turned and lobbed the iron straight at a man who'd emerged from the back stairwell of the house.

And hit him in the shoulder.

He let out a bawl of painful disbelief.

Eve didn't care. She pulled out of her best softball throw to date and ran. Her voice was tight, "*They have guns.*"

"*You don't say.*" Bethany panted. "And here I thought the wood panelling *split* in *solidarity.*"

The main stairs loomed ahead, and Candy turned onto them with a leap that left her legs and ankles stinging along her hamstrings.

"That's item 2 down the crapper," Eve leaned into running, and being an extremely fit volleyballer, caught hold of Bethany's less experienced run, and pulled as she turned. They almost crashed down the stairs.

"I bet they're all following us." Candy's teeth gritted in determination.

They spilled onto the main floor still in full charge, then plunged into a room's darkness again. They ran blind, guided only by Eve's memory of the spaces she pulled them through. Candy had caught a glimpse of a man's figure in the hall, fresh out of the kitchen doors. But he'd been nothing more than a blur. Was the room they'd arrived in a dead end, though? Candy thought so, but couldn't clearly recall, until Eve threw open a wood door, and they bungled out into a piano.

No. A Harpsicord, from the plinking sound it made.

Fleeing became a haze of gorgeous holiday décor and expensive furnishings until they found themselves in a room full of gaming systems. It was only then that Eve stopped, and Candy realized how far they'd run. They were in the same wing as the theatre seating and the pool house.

Bethany sank down to the floor in the shadow of a pool table and her breathing sounded like sobs where she huddled. It was piteous. Candy went to kneel beside her and threw her arm around the girl's shoulders for a squeeze. It wasn't much, and a bit awkward. But it was something. Then she sat on her heels. "Look. We're not dead yet."

Bethany pulled herself together to say, "That's not comforting, cheer-team."

Candy grinned. Like Eve, she was far from a cheerleader, "Putting aside that those guys shot at us, they're pretty tight with their radios. They don't leave them lying around." She got up and stretched. "If we can't tell anyone we're here because they've jammed wifi and Internet access, and somehow, I dunno how, cut off wireless access…. We're going to have to walk out of here. Past the dogs."

Bethany shook her head, "Why not just sit tight? Find a place to hide?"

"Because that works for, like, 1 or 2 people. That won't work for 25 who need regular bathroom breaks and, you know, have been drinking." Candy said.

"Shit." Eve murmured as she cooled off her muscles by pacing the room. She walked in the center, out of sight from the doors and the rows of windows. "I didn't think about that, *neek*. I mean, when she's sauced, all Clarissa does is *giggle*. She can hardly walk. How are we going to get the girls who've been hitting the liquor cabinet like a kettle drum out of this house? Quietly? I mean, if you think of Julia, and Candace, *alone-*"

Nope. Not thinking about it.

Candy was already feeling overwhelmed.

"Step 1 is Get back to Ivy's position." Candy told them. "We can't stay here. They could be doing a room-to-room search. You know. If they have any military background?"

"Again. *Catering*. Not exactly the people I expect would-"

Bethany crept out and stood up. "God, Eve, *they're not chefs*, okay? If they were, we'd have crab puffs and be polluted in the pool house, none the wiser, while they did... whatever."

"Well," Eve walked over to where Candy rested against a pinball machine she'd very much rather have been using. The tall, elegant girl caught one of Candy's tight, upright pigtails and tugged bits of moonlit splinter out of it to show them all, "Charlie's shooting – and I do think it was Charlie – isn't exactly the best taxpayer money can buy. So, no military for *him*."

"Sounded like the guy in charge wasn't exactly a big fan of Charlie's work either." Candy replied.

"We all know a bad boss can screw up your work. Especially the kiss up, kick down bosses. Maybe we'll luck out here, and Charlie will have been *careless*." Nodded Bethany, and both Eve and Candy looked at her. One because she'd *never* entertain having something as ordinary as *a day job*, and one because she'd had one from her earliest opportunity but had never expected one of the Waverleigh girls to know a thing about working.

"You've gotta try a bad *coach*, sometime, Bethany." Eve sighed. "I think there's a limit to how much screaming a boss can do in the office. No such thing on the court. Sometimes Devereaux actually *loses her voice*. Joke goes, that's how you know Waverleigh will win the next trophy."

Candy could only nod mutely at the assumptions she'd been making about these girls. She reached down and tugged her Ugly Sweater. "Next year, ask Ivy to spring for noise cancelling ear buds."

And, finally, Eve cracked a smile, "So either we can ignore the catering next year, or... I guess the earbuds wouldn't work without Internet and satellites and whatever, right *neek*?"

And Candy felt her back stiffen in sudden realization.

They were sitting in a chalet with *who knew* how much open land surrounding it, that had photos of Ivy with her family at a swanky, lake-side, log cabin, that Candy had assumed was somewhere in *Vale*, or Montana, or something. But what if that lake was somewhere out back of this sprawling house, safe and sound, protected from people? What if it was here on Chérubin land?

Then maybe, for safety's sake, Ivy's parents already have satellite phones on this property, maybe in that metal shed?

A dog exploded into barking somewhere inside the house and interrupted their separate thoughts.

Eve's eyes goggled. "Candy-land, I think I found your room-to-room search."

Bethany added to this, "That sure doesn't sound like Poupée."

Candy reached up to rub her eyes with the heels of her hands. "No, that sounds like a *hell beast*." Her night *couldn't get* any worse.

Her mother's words came back to her: *Rich people are nothing but trouble, baby. They think money solves all their problems, ah.*

She muttered the line, "*But can't imagine what causes them.*"

"What?" Bethany blinked at her.

"What do we do?" Eve asked breathlessly. The next tumbled out almost in time-lapse. "Full disclosure, I hate big dogs. My uncle had his girlfriend over while he was supposed to be minding me, and they watched *Cujo*."

"Weird." Candy said.

"Yep." Eve agreed.

"We need to get to Ivy's group." Candy turned them in the room and looked at the row of windows along an outdoor deck. "We need to go back the way we came." She was wishing for her leaky UGGs right about then.

Eve didn't need to be told twice. She went to the deck doors and unlocked them.

"Don't open them." Candy checked them for a door and window sensor, an entry alarm, anything. This door had a pair of small white boxes at the top, but... the little light she strained to make out seemed to have gone dark.

"Looks like Charlie brought the system down." Candy opened the door and no alarm sounded. "*All* the way down." She was met by the thump of cold air. It bit into her nose and mouth and made her eyes water. She looked down at their sock feet.

Bethany nodded across at Candy, her breaths already a twisting smoke in the cold air, "This is going to hurt."

Eve pushed through, "Maybe less than you think. Follow me."

They shut the door behind them and stepped out into the bite of 25 below in sweaters and sock feet. The pain was, for the first few minutes, the most immediate thing in Candy's world. Even trotting along the scrupulously cleared stone slab tile of the deck, her feet began to burn. Candy shook within the first few minutes, teeth chattering as she followed Eve's fast, willowy body through a torment of cold. Bethany slid and stumbled in the dark, and Candy's hand caught her elbow.

They huddled together and sped onward after Eve's indefatigable run.

Candy's eyes darted to the lawn in search of dogs. But none so far.

Then Eve stopped and they were able to catch up with her.

She shivered, just as they did, but with the determination of an Alpha athlete.

"Plan?" Candy ground out. "What's the plan?"

Eve opened her hands ahead of her. Only then did Candy see the guy smoking a cigarette outside a side door that was... open.

"No offense," Bethany shuddered, "but I would kick the God-fearing shit out of that man, myself, with the strength of a dozen men... for a cocoa and slippers, right now."

"Huddle." Candy said. She crouched and edged out to the long loops of decorative yew along the inside railing of the deck, and with some coaxing got it off its hooks. Wrapped and folded it wasn't a bad thing to stand on, she brought it back to the pillar of stone they hid behind and threw it down. "Get on this. Everyone stand on this."

Her voice was slurring a little.

It raised them off the cold stone a couple of inches at least. Then they huddled together.

Minus 25. That innocent tickle of wind brought their outdoor time down from 30 to between 10 and 20 minutes before frostbite set in. Candy eyed the man by the door and knew... he had a lighter. He had a coat. He had a way inside. But he also had a gun.

"We have to attack him." Her voice was grim.

Eve's lips compressed, she shuddered out, "I'm not a *cavewoman, neek.*"

"No. It's not possible, Candy. I've... I've never hit anyone before. I hardly ever even... shout at people." Bethany blinked into the dark little circle of faces. "Oh my God. What if we *hurt* him?"

For a moment, Candy stared at them.

Hurt him?

Candy exhaled at her sock feet in the yews. She had to rephrase things. "I have to attack him."

Both girls fell silent and stared at her.

"Hypothermia makes it hard to move, and hard to think." Candy told them. "We're getting it, right now. We can't wait for this guy. I have to attack him."

"With what?" Eve juddered, "Your C-Sh-Sharp code book?"

Candy reached between them, and her hand came back from the corner with a shovel. She looked at them both. "My dad... wasn't on the side of the angels. Not for a long time.... And for me not *everything* about that... was bad."

Bethany's face crumpled. "He could hurt you. You can't."

But Eve's chin rose a fraction. "Oh, something tells me... she can." Now Eve crouched low and looked around the corner. "Chain-smoker is facing away. Go now, *neek*."

The education Candy's father had considered critical was very different than what her mother treasured. Cleaning Waverleigh had been a crowning achievement for Byeol Young-MacCann. A banner moment wreathed in shiny paper stars, carried aloft by blue sparrows. She'd travelled, worked hard, schemed, and planned, for Candy to have the kind of career immigrant moms dreamt of – fulfilling, safe, full of money. *A better life*. Candy had learned all about that glowing world at her mother's knee, coming up. But the pilot light inside of her, long shut off, gave a sudden huff as she bit down on the pain and raced across that slab tile deck.

Casey MacCann, her father, had been a newcomer to America too, flying his life and family overseas, looking for a future that didn't compromise all his principles. Looking for peace, really. But with his connections, and... particular skills it had become easier, and necessary, to sacrifice dreams to put food on the table, especially when Candy had come along. At least, *at first*. Between the books and the hash-tag-BeautyTube, Casey had taught his little girl how to survive *his* world.

Candy cleared the railing and pulled up her numbed legs.

The tuck was imperfect. She was... in pain and numbed with cold.

She was rusty.

But Candy figured she could probably stick-fight in her sleep.

Her body made no more sound in air than an owl wing would as she dropped.

She leaned the shovel a little right mid-arch, to avoid truly risking his life.

Boom. She hit and the plastic top of the shovel broke off over the man's shoulder and hurtled, end over end, into the snow. He dropped like a sack of oranges, into a snowbank.

She heard Casey's voice, clearly, in her head.

Good girl. You found his off button.

Her dad.

Candy got up from her crouch, shuddering with cold.

Her hands felt numb taking the guy's radio and... gun. She wasn't *amazing* with guns. But she wasn't *terrible* either. Candy clicked the safety on and took down her backpack to tuck it in the front zipper pouch. She also took his fancy, blue-flame, lighter. It was engraved 'Merry Christmas, babe! Love, Sara'. She lit it up to feel the heat against her hands. When Eve and Bethany arrived, they wove a wide berth around Candy and the man in the snow before they rushed inside.

This... she'd sort of expected. It had been why she'd warned them she had to attack.

But Eve scurried back out with a packing blanket and wrapped it around Candy. "Come on. You're like... you look blue."

"We can't leave him. He'll die." Candy shuddered.

"What we can't leave is that stick." Eve picked it up from the snow. "Go inside. Me and Beth will take care of the thug."

Beth. Candy thought on her way to the door.

Sure enough, Bethany hurried by her, carrying packing blankets of her own. She reached out and gave Candy's hand a tweak in passing, but Candy didn't feel it through the numbness. She walked her pins and needles into the house and found what looked like a large mudroom. It was full of industrial-style closets and, her hunting around discovered, garden clothes. There were more shovels, and 30-pound buckets of de-icer. There were... coats. She pulled on one of the dark blue 'Helly' coats and looked at the line of winter crocs with something close to tears in her eyes.

Her socks weren't wet, the cold hadn't allowed for that. She held them in her hands and shook them out to get the snow dust off of them before she slid them back on and tried the furred crocs on her feet. One pair fit, and she took them, standing with an oversized coat keeping her warm, wrapped in a scarf she'd hunted up from a basket of discarded things, and mismatched gloves. Maybe... red and black? Hard to tell in the dark.

She checked the front zip of the backpack again.

When Eve and Bethany came in, they pulled the man on a few packing blankets. He now lay on his back, which meant they'd rolled him there. Once he was in the room, they threw the remaining packing blankets over him, including the one Candy had discarded on the floor. Then they dug into the coats and crocs themselves.

Candy glanced over his youngish face, took out her cell phone, and snapped a photo of him, even though she couldn't send it anywhere. Yet. "Okay. We leave him."

"Shouldn't we tie him up?" Bethany glanced over her shoulder. Her usually pacific expression was concealed by the darkness in the room.

"This isn't Murder She Wrote. We leave him. He's got something to keep him warm, the dirtbag. We leave him and go find Ivy. We're past the hour mark. She's going to start looking soon. We don't want her looking." Candy still felt light and jittery from the cold and the vault back into her past life, pre-Waverleigh.

She exhaled and held up the radio. "I turned it down, but I know where they're searching, and I know the front doors aren't locked."

"Oh that," Eve took her hand out of the pocket of the coat she wore, little more than a silhouette in the shadows, and shook a big ring of keys at Candy.

"Oh my God." Bethany said, and... flicked on a flashlight she hadn't had prior to being in the room. Keys. A servant-style master set of keys.

Candy didn't know what they were for but... she was thrilled. They looked like a cornucopia full of money to her. "Everyone have gloves and a hat?" Candy shivered. "Got scarves?"

Bethany went back for a hat and gloves.

They went outside into the night.

The trick to this was to weave among the yews and stay amid the many tracks left by dogs and men walking around in the snow. Eve carried the broken wood handle of the shovel that Candy had used. She held it in one hand, and up along her shoulder, like one might carry a rifle if it wasn't broken open. But it was more of a security blanket than a weapon now that Candy had upped her game. They turned along the side of the house more exposed to wind and discovered it was blowing a steady 5 mph. Too cold for even the dogs to operate out here.

"We need to get inside. The windchill is, like, probably below 40." Candy said. She was fresh from checking the radio, and very anxious. Inside, the dogs had someone's scent up on the second floor. 'The caterers' were heading Westward in the house – the same direction they were walking along on the outside at the moment.

"We're close." Eve promised. She led them around dark, thick windows, and started jingling keys as she tried a door lock. It took close to 3 precious minutes in the deep freeze to find the correct one. But they stepped inside a room that was wrapped in warm, damp heat, and... flush with young women who had, long ago, changed out of their bathing suits, and back into their leggings, party dresses, and ugly sweaters.

"Is... is this the pool house?" Candy whispered.

Eve's voice made a low, but excited, "*Tah-dah*."

"Idiot." Bethany chortled in quiet response. Both girls grinned then.

The young women knew there was someone new in the room with them and didn't look happy about it. Candy couldn't describe their moonlit faces as petrified, though there *was* fear. They looked coldly furious instead. Resentful.

She stepped into the moonlit room, undid her scarf, and pulled back her hood. "Okay. So, who's ready to bail on this party?"

Astonishment blew through the gathered girls as Eve and Bethany came out of the shadows, hoods back, faces welcoming, broken stick and all.

Carol stood up immediately. "Where's Belle?"

"Working on getting you coats and boots so you can leave, right now." Candy said.

"What's going on?" Julia, with her head full of natural banana curls, climbed to her feet.

"Girl, why aren't you drunk?" Eve asked her.

"Shut up, my bitch. Gunmen harsh a buzz." Julia waved the comment off.

Eve chuckled at this, and only then noticed that Candy had peeled away to listen to the radio she'd stolen. She had her head bowed to it like a phone, as she'd turned it down. And while Bethany organized the girls to take final washroom trips, collect and fill their bottled water containers, and bring her a few fresh pads, Eve followed Candy toward the snowy windows. They were covered in Christmas lights that had probably blinked to the festive beat of Nat King Cole earlier tonight. Now they were as dark as a holiday horror story – *may your days be eerie and blight.*

"What?" Eve asked.

"They're chasing someone… right now." Candy's heartbeat cranked. She couldn't be there. Her eyes landed on the wood staff Eve carried. She wanted nothing more than to swing at these men. *Hard.* Instead, she stood stock still and listened with a sick feeling spreading in her middle, as the messages turned from 'in pursuit' to 'got her'. When that happened, she felt a swirl of light-headed sweat that nearly buckled her knees.

"What is it?" Eve edged in on her. Then Eve caught her and nearly kept her upright. "Candy?"

For a moment, she couldn't speak. She was listening on the line.

Listening for a shot. Listening for any kind of a clue.

When nothing came but, 'Get her down here' from the boss, she felt ill.

Voice hushed, she turned to Eve. "They have… one of us."

She couldn't describe the look of horror that passed over Eve's face, and never wanted to see such a thing again. They were still locked in this liminal shock when Ivy came in.

She rolled the wall between the Chérubin movie theatre and the pool house open. Easy.

Ivy tugged along three red sacks, furred at the top in white. They were heavy, so that she dragged them along the wood floor like an arctic explorer her sled. She only stopped when she saw Candy and Eve staring at her from the moonlight. She dropped the sacks and coats and boots tumbled out on the pool deck. "Eve? Candy? Where's Bethany?"

Eve stepped up, "Herding the girls for a final pee."

In fact, Bethany had hurried out at the sound of Ivy's voice, and stood, wordlessly searching the darkness behind the girl.

Chelsea came into the moonlight. She pulled three more red bags by their woven wool strings, behind her. Her voice wobbled as she stopped, "Look at that. *Ho', ho', ho'.*"

Eve's smile broadened. "Oh, shut-up, Chelsea. You just *think* that's funny."

It was Candy who stepped out and looked over the spill of boots and coats. Her expression, she knew, was grave, "Do we have enough?"

Ivy, her hair bedraggled and her eyes, frankly, red with crying, noted, "I supplemented from closets. I have one, maybe two spare coats? Three pairs extra of boots. And three pairs of slippers. Now what?"

Bethany and Eve drew in, and the latter girl held up the ring of keys. "How about that corrugated steel car collection your dad has, about quarter-mile down your driveway? I know for a fact he keeps that heated bitch locked tight. And it's hard to break through a steel wall."

Candy nodded. "Your dad built a fort on your property. Don't let it go to waste now that you need it. You're going to make a break for it."

Now, Bethany looked aside at her. "*You're* going to make a break for it?" She shook her head.

"Yeah. You are. All of you." Candy told them. She took the broken shovel handle from Eve and shrugged off her oversized coat, "There's something I've got to do."

Ivy didn't hesitate to swap coats with her, grim-faced the whole time. She took the oversized Helly Hensen coat and her lips compressed as the girls began to drift back into the pool room. They found the Santa Claus sacks of their coats and boots and scrambled through them hungrily.

Then Ivy tugged Chelsea's and Bethany's sleeves. The young hostess looked grey. "Ladies... you have to help me tell Carol... that those maniacs have Belle. She gave us her bags and just... ran in the opposite direction to distract those men.... So, we could get to you. We weren't going to make it."

Then... everything would have fallen apart.

Little, perfectionist Belle, with her schedules and clock-work mind, had glimpsed the future of this venture. What could happen to the many, because of the failure of the few. And she'd stepped up and taken the hit. Candy was stunned. And a bit *awed*.

She was also, at her steely core, set on repayment.

Beside her, Bethany's hands had clapped over her mouth in a sudden fracture of reaction. "Oh no. Oh shit. *Belle*."

"Be cool. It's not going to be for long." Candy zipped the red coat she'd taken from Ivy and picked up her bag. "I'm going to go get her back."

"Oh yeah?" And how are you going to do that? Chelsea hugged herself. "Those guys are monsters, Candy. You don't understand. They came after the three of us when we were sneaking the clothes through the back halls. And when one of them got too close, Poupée bit a guy. We got away, but he shot at her. They could have *killed* her. It's a miracle she got out of there."

Silence.

They'd shot at her too. Candy knew the feeling.

Off on Candy's left, Eve started sniffling. Because she was crying. "I mean... is she okay?"

"She ran away. There was no... blood." Ivy swabbed her cheek. "I think so. Just...."

Candy's emotions... felt numb as a sleeping limb. Who shot at a little dog? Same guys as had their hands on Belle, right now.

Julia, now dressed for the outside, stood nearby, horrified. "What the hell? She's. A. *Puppy.*"

Veins stood out in Ivy's temples. She was under terrible pressure to maintain control, but muscled through it to mutter a tight, "Yes. And... and that's not even the worst of it. Now they have-"

A wail rose from the girl's washroom, quite separate from the silence that had fallen among the decorations in the warm pool room. Several of the girls jumped.

"Quiet her down." Candy exhaled.

Chelsea wheeled around, "It's *Carol.*"

"How does she already know?" Ivy hastily wiped her tears from her cheeks.

But it wasn't some strange twin connection, or, not this time. Carol hurried over carrying her twin's coat and boots. "Where is she? Ivy, where *is* she?"

Candy bit down on her woe, "She's trapped upstairs. And I'm going to get her."

"*How?*" Ivy sobbed.

Candy laid down the stick, unzipped the front of the bag, and pulled out the gun. That caught attention. When she chambered a round, the snap of the slide echoed in the huge room. It was a large Glock and would have a lot more recoil. But Candy had fired bigger. She knew her wrists could take the wallop. At least *for a while*. Her dad had taught her how to do it, and... she was simply *built that way*.

The girls stood still in all stages of outdoor dress. Carol was speechless.

"Put Belle's coat and boots in a bag and leave this to me." Candy said bleakly. "Go."

"You're going to get yourself killed." Ivy hissed.

"Yeah, well, they're bringing Belle to the kitchen, and I don't know why they'd do that. They might think she's the one, or *knows* the one of us, who was in their network. They might think she's been causing trouble and would be a pretty good example for the rest of us. Big boss is kinda steamed about what we've been doing. Ivy, I've been running through your house all night. I know how to get to the kitchen." Candy told her. "And I know how to use a gun."

Eve wiped her face and blinked awake. "*Trust me*. She can do this. If anyone can." She handed over the ring of keys to Ivy. "And she won't be alone. *I'm* going to help her."

Candy took out the laptop and waved it at them. "Your dad's garage has its own network. We need to get over there and video call *everyone*. And Eve, you're not coming with me."

"*Yes, I am*." Said the girl.

"No." Ivy blinked. "No, you're not. You're the most competitive, most driven, longest-legged queen-bee of us all. And you're the track team's golden girl. *No one* is a faster runner." Ivy handed back the ring of keys with one selected and pinched between her thumb and forefinger. The key had a white plastic ring around the grip. "And this will get you in the door."

Then Candy zipped the laptop away and handed the girl the backpack. "So. How fast can you run a quarter of a mile on a cleared driveway, Eve?"

She took the bag and pulled it onto her back in resignation. "We're going to find out. Chelsea? Make sure everyone's ready to head out behind me. *Everyone* runs. Even if they suck at it."

Bethany, who, in fact, *did* suck at running, nodded. "We're going to leave a great big trail through the snow until we reach the ploughed road. So... everyone keeps an eye on everyone else."

"*No chick left behind.*" Chelsea said and looked at Candy. "Do you hear me?"

She only nodded.

It took only 2 minutes of prep from there. The girls lined up in twos and threes, with the decent runners monitoring the bad. Candy watched them. Eve stood by the door, waggling her long arms and legs and checking her watch by its light. She zipped her pocket around the keys.

"Candy?"

She looked to see Carol with Ivy. The twin girl's expression was stark... an eerie, being that she wasn't Belle. She'd been speaking, "Your dad was a criminal? He's in prison? Is that true?"

She felt a flush of heat that she ignored, and Candy said, "He was a criminal. He went to prison. Then he went straight." She told the girl. She didn't get to see her dad much anymore. But he wasn't up the river. He just... couldn't live with himself, not when it came to his family, and the spectre of disappointment and shame he imagined he'd caused them.

Her lips compressed in a tight nod, "Did he teach you stuff?" Carol asked.

"He did."

Now Carol's dark eyes went sharp. "Will you do that stuff to get my sister back?"

Candy turned in place, to fully face the girl, and she felt herself harden inside. "I will use *everything I've got* to get your sister back."

"Good." Carol's voice was hoarse with tears. "Do that. I'll give you anything. *Anything.*"

Ivy pulled the girl away and into line and glanced back over her shoulder as she did so.

Just seconds later, they all went still and quiet, as they'd been instructed to do when they were ready. Just like that, Eve stepped out into the night and started running through the drifted path that led toward the driveway. She had explosive speed and was gone from sight in a matter of seconds. Silently, the girls pulled out into the night in a line of twos and threes, behind her.

And Candy was alone.

She picked up the red sack at her feet and slung it over her shoulder. Gun naked in one hand, she made for the open wall to the theatre room.

It was an almost... out of body experience, having a *plan* for a moment like this one.

But she did.

Step 1. Only take the back rooms and servants halls.

By this means, she found, and skirted the *glorious* Wedgewood Christmas tree. It had to be close to 15 feet tall in a main room straight out of the Nutcracker, with a grand piano, cello – Ivy was in band – and a fireplace so large and tall, Candy might have strung a hammock in it and paid rent. She skulked through these huge rooms feeling smaller and smaller, herself, while she was hiding. While she worked on *becoming invisible.* And if she willed herself so, who were the rats in the kitchen, to tell her No?

A dog barked in the hall, but it was beyond closed doors.

She switched the gun between hands to wipe away sweat from her palms.

Candy was dressed for outside in this big, winterized house.

But felt stone cold.

Until the little head poked out from around a corner ahead of her. Then some of the tension let up a little. "*Dolly*. Hi, Dolly." The little dog waggled her way over, in that way of puppies, where their entire body wiggled with joy.

"You can't come with me where I'm going." Candy side-stepped and carried the pup into a piano room. She briefly stood there, looked at the old upright... and wished all this wasn't happening. But that did nothing to help Belle. So, she gave the puppy a nod. "Try not to do any of your French name on the carpet while we're away, okay?"

She sat down and wagged her tail as Candy stepped out and shut the door.

Speaking of dogs. Step 2. Distract any dogs.

She arrived in a room with an upright freezer and double fridge.

There, Candy took out every left-over she could find and laid the platters around in inconspicuous places in the halls and rooms. *Nothing distracts a dog like their stomach*, her mom always said. While it was debatable if Byeol was being rhetorical or not, she hadn't made it up.

Candy hid when she heard men coming.

One of them had a dog on a lead, who immediately started to become fractious.

"What is up with you?" he tugged the choke chain tight enough for the dog to cough. Then, when the dog complained... he kicked it. Where Candy could *see*. Her eyes jumped from the cry and whimper up to the shithead full of suppressed rage.

He didn't deserve the power conferred by such a dog. But wishing it would turn and tear the ass right out of the guy's pants wasn't getting anyone anywhere.

Next, Candy made it into the butler's pantry, which was risky. But the darkness and the anger had also made Candy bold. She sat with her legs curled up and spread the Santa Claus sack around her so that she was a lumpy, hidden thing in one corner, just under the stove. They had light in the next room. She didn't want it to ruin her night vision. Not if she could avoid it.

In the kitchen opposite her, men burst into a sudden volley of laughter.

"So, power and cellular service is down from Waverleigh Estates to the third-to-last house on Millionaire row." Charlie said. "Seven houses total are empty for the Holidays. We've got four teams and about 10 hours till daylight. We are *golden*."

Glasses... *clinked*. For real.

"Nicely done. Nicely done." Came the nearly vibrating voice that she knew as 'Boss'. "How are the other teams doing?"

A new guy laughed, "So, Jimmy and Simon have just about ransacked the Goldman's on Lot E already. The team in the Darcy's house thinks they'll be done next. And that means you're losing the betting pool, Charlie."

"I got the money." Charlie said, and laughter swelled. When the noise died a little, he added. "We'll all have the money, soon enough." Another swell, this one accompanied by the arrival of more men. Candy had lost count of how many she estimated were inside the big kitchen. She reached up and pulled down her beanie, then tugged the scarf up over most of her face.

She laid the gun down against her belly and flexed her hands and wrists under the sack. *Relax.*

"Stop it!" Belle snapped as she came into earshot.

"What have we here?" Boss asked.

"We caught her." Said a deeper voice, proudly. "The one causing *all* the trouble."

Under the red velvet Candy thought: *Not yet.*

There was a fleshy noise, like they slung Belle into the room, and she collided with cupboards, punctuated by the whining of a dog. But the men found it all funny.

"So... *you're* the tough girl." Boss said into the silence that followed.

Clink. He set down a glass.

Candy couldn't see her, but Belle didn't say a word.

"You're the little fool who dared to fiddle with my plan. Muck about in the network I told Charlie to take down. Hard. *You* led our dogs on a goose-chase though the house, like we were a bunch of clowns. *You wasted our valuable time.*" Boss sounded angry. "*Is that right?*"

"Yes, that's right." Belle's voice throbbed with anger at them. "That was *me*. *All* of it. And you deserve worse. *Much* worse." Candy remembered that Belle had seen them shoot at Ivy's little dog. She didn't expect much out of these idiots either.

"Well, if you cause trouble for me and mine, I cause trouble for you and yours." Boss said. "Those are biblical rules, and it's Christmas, my dear. An eye for an eye."

Yep. Got it. Candy got to her feet and shook herself to readiness. She picked up the Santa sack.

Step 3. Mug... the thieves.

"What? Are you *stupid* or something? Those other girls had nothing to do with it." Belle was bluffing like a Theatre Arts major. "They're... *soft*. Their brains are full of fluff and hair salons and mani-pedis. But their parents are powerful and... vengeful. You'd be smart to leave them out of all of this, and not make things *even worse* for, uh, you and yours. *It could be. If you get my drift.*"

Several of the men laughed at her.

For Candy, time slowed down. She knew where in the room Belle was, by where her voice had come from. She'd been waiting for 'Boss' to talk again. And now he did.

His voice seemed to stretch in her head. He said, "No, I don't 'get your drift.'"

Candy stepped out around the corner, red coat, black gun, red bag, and her face all but covered. She whipped up her gloved hand. By way of hello, Candy pulled the trigger and shot a guy in the shoulder. He went down with a howl.

Into the shocked silence, Candy snarled, "She means *me*."

A slug hit the next guy that moved, passed through his forearm, and hit the gong above the stove with a rattling belling before it bounced around the room. Belle broke and ran into the hall. She sure as hell knew Candy's voice when she heard it.

Candy's speech stream bifurcated, low, calm, and kind for Belle, and nothing short of savage for the men. "*Go-go-go.*" She told Belle. "Merry Christmas," she shouted at the men, "I know how to shoot."

The gun roared. The gong belled. The ricochet whined around the room. Finally, they had the presence of mind to dive for cover among the counters and cutting boards.

Candy backed up a few steps as the thug let go the dog's lead. "Get her boy!"

But the dog tore by her and behind a potted miniature Christmas tree down by the pantry. Candy had left half a pot roast there, and it had been a long night. "Shouldn't keep him so hungry, loser." Candy made her way down the hall shooting at an angle, so she could hit the gong, so it would sound the bell, and the room was *painted* with shrapnel and ricochet.

Her father had done something like this before on a heist. He's started out in muggings.... She'd heard the story.

Her back touched Belle and they turned and ran.

Seven shots gone, of 15 rounds.

She heaved the red bag to Belle. "Your coat and boots."

They spilled onto the main stairs and took a right along the map in Candy's memory. She counted 4 doors before she entered a room, rushed to the window, and threw up the sash there. And outside lay the moonlit snowbank, like a sledding hill, just as she remembered. "Get dressed," she looked back into the room. "*Wha?!*"

The caterer's German Shepard looked at her. He still had part of the pot roast in his jaws and was trying hard to wolf it down. "*Jesus*, Belle."

"I couldn't leave him." She shoved on her boots on the bed, the end of the short lead in her teeth. "I – honest to God – I couldn't leave him."

"Can you get him out the window?" Candy asked, heard a sound, and turned to take a double grip on the gun she pointed at the door.

Her arm was throbbing from absorbing the shots she'd one-handed downstairs. But no one came for her to shoot at.

Instead... she thought she heard a thin, faraway... music outside.

It surprised her when Belle scooted by, climbed on the sill, and turned back to say, "Come on, buddy!" She jumped to the bank of snow and slid down and the dog went merrily along with.

This was, for Belle, the worst moment. She picked up the red velvet bag, tucked the gun in it, wound it around her wrist, and... leapt out of the second-floor window. Without the gun at the ready, she felt exposed and small. But she slid down to the pathway and Belle, without any undue harm done. She did admonish the girl, "Your sister is *freaking out.*"

Belle's laugh hid a gurgle of tears inside it, but she nodded. "Where is she?"

"Quarter of a mile down the driveway in a steel building. And we're gonna run." Candy took the gun out and ran with it. She heard the crack of a shot from the front of the house as she broke for the driveway. It shook the snow off a noble fir close by as they passed.

But she had, she realized as she turned, crouched, and fired at the foot of a running man, *trained* to shoot with her dad. They'd gone to the range a lot in her youth, and she'd graduated, gun to gun, for years.

As much as it hurt to shoot this one, she would.

The man spilled into the snow and curled into a wailing ball around his foot.

When she looked, Belle and the dog were well ahead of her. In her white coat, Belle made a poor target in the snow too.

Red was easier.

Candy launched after through a sudden hail of gunfire from the front and flank of the house but passed into trees around the bend in the drive. It took 8 minutes with the dodging and shooting she had to do, to reach the garage. It reared out of the snow, red as a cardinal's breast, solid steel, and capped in more of the same. The windows were shuttered in metal. There wasn't as much as a ladder outside in the snow. It gave every appearance of being impregnable. *Apart from the half open garage door in the front.*

She waved at the girls who peeked from inside and beckoned at her. "Go. Go! Get in! Shut the-"

But they didn't, or didn't hear her, even as she ran up to them and did an impressive slide into home-base – if she had to say so herself – because the steel door had begun to roll down above her.

When the door was shut, and the locks turned into place, Candy closed her eyes. She lay on the epoxy floor on her back and panted, gun across her chest, opposite hand over the grip, and her finger carefully away from the trigger.

When she opened her eyes again... she was ringed by young women's faces and bent figures silhouetted by the emergency lighting overhead.

"You all right there, Candy MacCann?" Eve – who was one of them – asked.

"I... I only have 4 rounds left in this—" but the thin strains of music resolved into the sound... of sirens wailing along the road from Waverleigh into Millionaire row.

Carefully, Candy sat up on the epoxy, clicked the safety, and tucked the gun into the velvet bag. "The cops are gonna love me. The daughter of a felon... shooting at a bunch of criminals... robbing Millionaire row, by the way."

"Yeah. It's almost like you're a *hero*." Ivy said as she pushed into the girls around her, and draped Candy in a red blanket that said BMW.

"They can't find me with this." Candy set down the bag.

"With what?" Asked Bethany.

"The *gun*." Candy said with some emphasis, but when she looked, the red velvet bag had been whisked away and she sat on the heated floor... with just the powder burns on her mismatched gloves. She took them off, and Ivy snatched them up.

"Eve?"

"Yes, dear?"

"Would you burn these?"

"It's Christmas, it's the time for roasting things on an open fire. So, of course." Eve tucked in and caught up the red one, and the green, so dark it had looked black in the dark.

Belle and Carol broke apart to help her to her feet again, which was good, because Candy was cold and sore as they brought her to an area full of couches that circled a pot-bellied stove. Her former gloves were peeling and vanishing into the flames even as she sat down among them pillows.

Then Belle laughed, "You know hiding what you've done is paranoia, right?"

"Maybe." Candy's eyes followed Julia as she set a cast iron kettle on to boil. The dog milled around behind her, lost in the big open room. "I mean I'm not the only criminal here now, am I."

"What do you mean?" Ivy sat down beside her as Candy unwound the scarf that hid her face, and that had concealed the blood on her lip. Candy had bitten it leaping from the window and landing in the snowbank.

"I mean *Belle*. She stole their dog." Candy indicated the big animal, who, even now, crouched and skulked away out of reach of kicks that weren't, and would never again, come. "Speaking of which, I found Poopsy. She's not hurt, not that I could see. But she is locked in a piano room near the kitchen, being a good girl. I hope."

"Candy... it's called... a recital room," Ivy said. But the sentence had been hard to get through, and Ivy had to cover her face with her hands for a moment. Several of the other girls hugged her.

"There's hot chocolate in your dad's breakroom." Eve reappeared. "And—!" She waggled a bottle of Baileys at the room full of girls. *That* got cheers among the tears.

"You okay?" Bethany ducked in to ask. "You look... not okay."

Candy couldn't lie, there was a lot of personal history wrapped up in a bow and delivered in the dry words: "When I hear sirens... sirens make me *tense*."

Bethany stayed, sitting on the couch in silent support.

Chelsea smiled brightly, "Ah, well, there *is* something we can do about that."

When they left her, Candy sat staring at the cast-iron stove, numbly. She wondered... where the gun was. She'd liked that gun, even if it had been too big for her hand. Maybe she could grow into a gun like that one.

She also wondered if the police would suspect *a McCann* tipped this criminal gang off about Millionaire row to begin with. She'd had run-ins with them before in other places when they'd found out who she was. Her father had become a conman, after all, and had pulled some real Ocean's 8 shit in her lifetime, enough that F.B.I. and police knew his name.

However, after a while she mostly listened to the sound of sirens vanish behind a wall... of music, and watched Ivy slip miniature marshmallows to the massive, and very frightened, dog.

But the fear would pass.

He would learn, given time with Ivy, that she was truly a good person. Just as Candy had.

She knew the police would make it down here soon enough. She'd try to avoid questioning. Maybe she'd just hide in the back of one of the cars here? She shut her eyes feeling tired.

But better. Behind her, girls worked through a new key ring. They went from car to car to turn on the radios to the same station, so that the whole garage echoed in the firelight: '*Ho-ho-ho, who wouldn't go? / Ho-ho-ho, who wouldn't go? / Up on the house-top, click-click-click / Down through the chimney with good Saint Nick*'.

And that, Candy could handle.

Author's Note

Thanks for reading! I hope you enjoyed this book. If you did, leave a review at your favourite retailer site. Reviews help writers (like me!) attract readers (like you), and they give authors your helpful feedback on their work. You may not know this, but reviews help push authors up in the algorithms for book-selling sites like Amazon or Book Bub. Without that kind of visibility, authors and books—even the ones you love the most—just fade away.

Your support keeps authors in the business of writing. I hope the reviews you write give you a warm-fuzzy feeling you're doing something good for a book you love, and an author whose months and years of lonesome work you appreciate! **Your review matters to writers!**
Join me for adventures in my other novels available online in many formats (from ebook to audiobook)!
Join my Advanced Review Copy (ARC) team to get books for free in exchange for a fair review wherever you buy books!
https://www.tracyeire.site/joinforces
https://www.facebook.com/tracy.eire.writer/
and join my newsletter at the bottom of this page
https://www.tracyeire.site/books
Thank you!

Join me for *Cardinal Machines*! It's like **Veronica Mars** meets **Detroit: Become Human** with a healthy dose of **Die Hard!**

https://books2read.com/Cardinal-Machines

Series and Singles

The Cardinal Machines series
Book 01 - https://books2read.com/Cardinal-Machines
Book 02 - https://books2read.com/Cardinal-Spark
Book 03 - https://books2read.com/Cardinal-Ignition
Book 04 - https://books2read.com/Cardinal-Light
Book 05 - https://books2read.com/Cardinal-Summit
Book 06 - https://books2read.com/Cardinal-Soul

The Folded Earth series
Book 01 - https://books2read.com/Folded-Earth
Book 02 - https://books2read.com/Twisted-Cord
Book 03 - https://books2read.com/Tempered-Fire

The Rath of Shelter Island (short story and audiobook)
https://books2read.com/The-Rath-of-Shelter-Island
Hard Candy (novella and audiobook)
https://books2read.com/Hard-Candy
Wings & Justice (novella)
https://books2read.com/WingsAndJustice
Stars in Legions (novella)
https://books2read.com/Stars-in-Legions